PiNK PANTHER

and

SONS

Fun at the Picnic

By Sandra Beris

Illustrated by David Gantz

A GOLDEN BOOK • NEW YORK

Western Publishing Company, Inc., Racine, Wisconsin 53404

TM & © 1985 United Artists Corporation. All rights reserved. Printed in the U.S.A. by Western Publishing Company, Inc. No part of this book may be reproduced or copied in any form without written permission from the publisher. GOLDEN®, GOLDEN & DESIGN®, A GOLDEN BOOK®, and A LITTLE GOLDEN BOOK® are trademarks of Western Publishing Company, Inc. Library of Congress Catalog Card Number: 85-70339   ISBN 0-307-02031-2   A B C D E F G H I J

The Pink Panther patted his bow tie into place. "I'm trusting you to take care of Panky at the Fall Picnic today," he told his son Pinky. "Keep an eye on him, and don't let him run off by himself."

The Pink Panther put on his pink top hat and his pink silk cape. He smiled at his own pink face in the mirror.

"Oh, Pop! Why won't you tell us what you're going to do for the Picnic Surprise Show?" Pinky asked.

"Because it's a surprise," said the Pink Panther. "You'll find out tonight."

Pinky sighed. He wanted to do the things his famous father did. "Say, Pop, can't I be in the show, too?" he asked.

"If you take extra-good care of Panky, maybe you can."
The Pink Panther smiled. "Just make sure you and Panky
are around when the show starts."

And with a wink, the Pink Panther went out the door.

No sooner had he gone than Panky began to wail. "Me wanna go picnic!" He wanted to play games and climb trees and eat ice cream.

"We'll go when the others get here," Pinky said. "But remember, you'll have to be good and do what I say."

Just then the doorbell rang, and in marched Pinky's friends the Rainbow Panthers—Chatta, Anney O'Gizmo, Rocko, Murfel, and Punkin. They were all looking forward to the picnic.

"Let's get going," said Rocko. "I want to find out what the surprise is in the Picnic Surprise Show. Did your pop tell you?"

"No," Pinky said. "I guess we'll just have to wait and see, like everyone else." He didn't tell them that he might be in the show.

"We'll find out tonight," Chatta said. "Now come on, you guys, or we won't get to the picnic at all!"

The group started off. Pinky held Panky's hand. "You stay close to me," he ordered. "Try to be a good boy at the picnic, and no running around."

The Rainbow Panthers soon arrived at the park. Crowds of people were already there, and everyone seemed to be doing something exciting. They were bicycling, roller-skating, and even flying kites.

The friends wanted to see everything. First they followed their noses to the picnic tables. There they found barbecued chicken, lemonade, and, best of all, pistachio ice cream.

"Green ice cream! Me want!" said Panky.

"Later," said Pinky.

Then the friends walked to the lake. It looked all dressed up for the picnic. Lights sparkled in the trees around it, and boats bobbed on the water.

"Me wanna boat ride!" said Panky.

"No!" said Pinky.

The group walked to the playground. "Let's play
basketball," Rocko said.

"That's a great idea!" Anney said.

But when the Rainbow Panthers turned around, there were Finko the Fang and his friends the Howl's Angels. The Rainbow Panthers and the Howl's Angels all lived on the same street. But they didn't always get along.

"Basketball, anyone?" Finko challenged.

Pinky made Panky sit down nearby. "Stay put!" he said. Then he led the Rainbow Panthers onto the court.

The Rainbow Panthers did their best at basketball.
With their great team spirit, they soon won the game.
"Yaaayyyy, Pinky!" they cried, cheering their best player.

Finko was angry that his team had lost. He stomped up
and down.

"What a sore loser!" Chatta thought, turning away.

"Pinky!" cried Chatta. "Panky is gone!"

"Oh, no!" Pinky said. He remembered what his father had said, and he remembered that the Surprise Show was about to start. He had to think fast. "We'd better split up to look for him," he said. "Chatta, try the picnic tables. Murfel and Punkin, the playground. Rocko, the bandstand. Anney, stay here to see if Panky comes back. We'll all meet at the bandstand in time for the show."

Pinky ran to look for Panky at the boat dock. Sure enough, there was Panky, climbing into a rowboat.

Pinky pulled him out. "Panky, you are a very bad boy!"

Panky knew that he should not have run off alone. But he felt so unhappy that all he said was, "Pinky, you a mean boy!"

Pinky didn't know what to say. For the first time that day, he thought about how little fun Panky was having at the picnic.

"Maybe I *have* been a little too bossy," Pinky admitted. "I'll tell you what—I'll bring you back tomorrow for a boat ride."

And for the first time that day, Panky grinned.

"Now let's go and see Pop!" Pinky said, and they headed for the show.

The friends were happy to have Panky back. "The show is going to start any minute," Chatta said. "I can't wait to see what the surprise is."

But when she turned to look at Pinky, he wasn't there! "Now Pinky's disappeared!" she told the others.

But there was no time to search for him. Suddenly a deep voice boomed over the loudspeaker.

"Ladies and gentlemen! The Fall Picnic is proud to present the Surprise Show, starring the Pink Panther!"

The Pink Panther smiled and bowed. "I'll bet you're all wondering what the first surprise will be," he said. "Well, I know you were expecting to end your day with a Pink Panther. But were you expecting to end it with…"

"...*two* Pink Panthers?"

When he opened his cape, out popped Pinky in a silk cape of his own. The Rainbow Panthers were surprised to see their leader onstage. But Pinky was happy to be there, dancing beside his dad while the crowd cheered.